A Lesson About Jealousy

# Pippa
## Learns to Share the Spotlight

**The Daystar Dogs**

**SISSY GOFF & DAVID THOMAS**
Illustrated by Ghyslaine Vaysset

**BETHANY HOUSE**
a division of Baker Publishing Group
Minneapolis, Minnesota

## Books by Sissy Goff from Bethany House Publishers

*Raising Worry-Free Girls*
*Braver, Stronger, Smarter*
*Brave*
*The Worry-Free Parent*
*The Worry-Free Parent Workbook*

## Books by David Thomas from Bethany House Publishers

*Raising Emotionally Strong Boys*
*Strong and Smart*

*Are My Kids on Track?* by Sissy Goff, David Thomas, and Melissa Trevathan

## The Daystar Dogs

*Owen Learns He Has What It Takes* by David Thomas
*Lucy Learns to Be Brave* by Sissy Goff
*Pippa Learns to Share the Spotlight* by Sissy Goff and David Thomas
*Happy Finds Her Calm* by Sissy Goff and David Thomas

© 2025 by Helen S. Goff and David Scott Thomas

Published by Bethany House Publishers
Minneapolis, Minnesota

BethanyHouse.com

Bethany House Publishers is a division of
Baker Publishing Group, Grand Rapids, Michigan

Printed in China

All rights reserved. No part of this publication may be reproduced, stored in a retrieval system, or transmitted in any form or by any means—for example, electronic, photocopy, recording—without the prior written permission of the publisher. The only exception is brief quotations in printed reviews.

ISBN: 9780764243479 (cloth)
ISBN: 9781493451203 (ebook)

25  26  27  28  29  30  31     7  6  5  4  3  2  1

Library of Congress Cataloging-in-Publication Control Number: 2025010669

The information in this book is intended solely as an educational resource, not as a tool to be used for medical diagnosis or treatment. The information presented is in no way a substitute for consultation with a personal health care professional. Readers should consult their personal health care professional before adopting any of the suggestions in this book or drawing inferences from the text. The author and publisher specifically disclaim all responsibility for any liability, loss, or risk, personal or otherwise, which is incurred as a consequence, directly or indirectly, of the use of and/or application of any of the contents of this book.

Art direction by Jennifer Parker
Typesetting and design by Jane Klein
Illustrated by Ghyslaine Vaysset

The authors are represented by Alive Literary Agency, AliveLiterary.com.
The illustrator is represented by Gwen Walters Artist Representative.

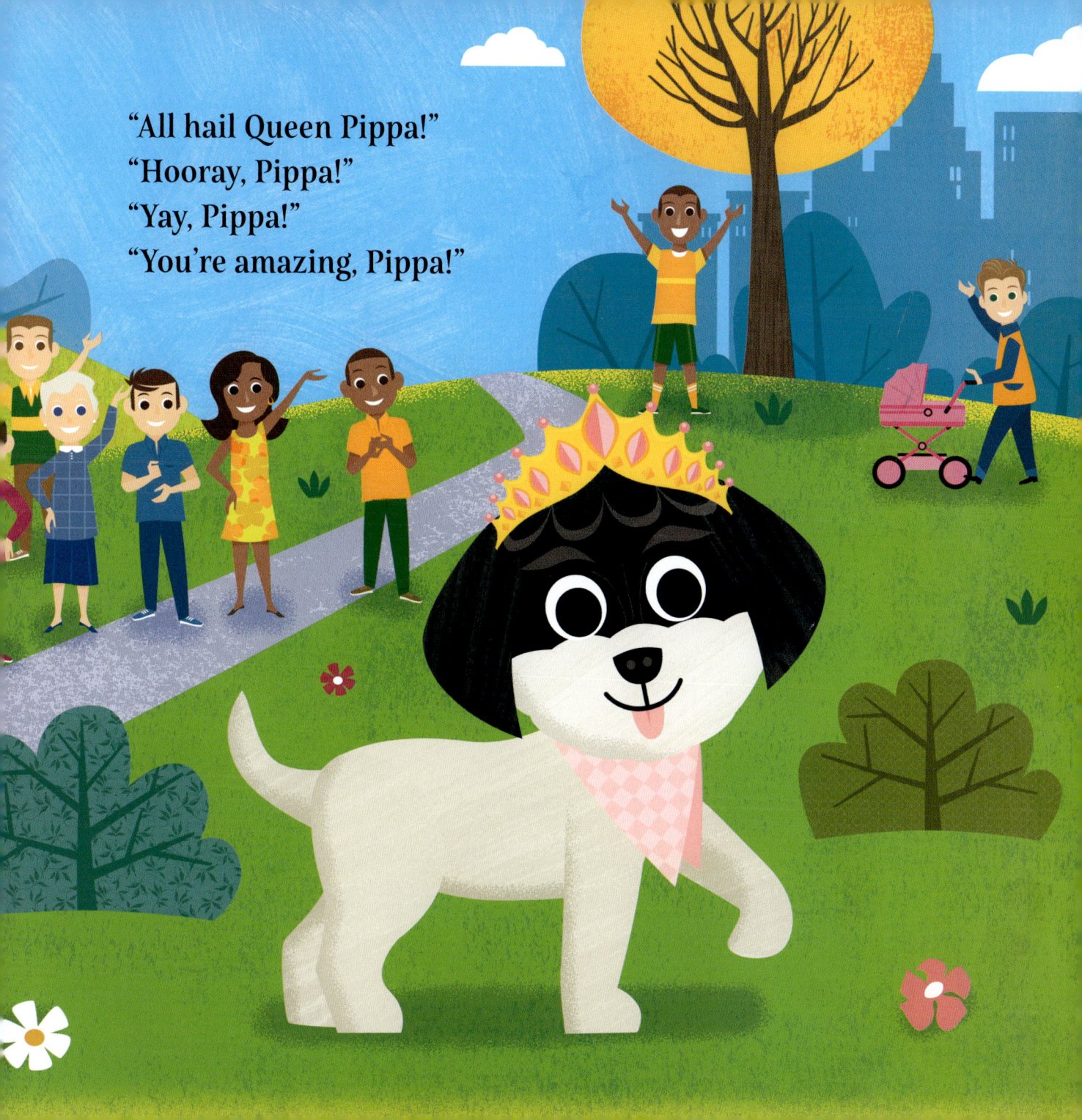

"All hail Queen Pippa!"
"Hooray, Pippa!"
"Yay, Pippa!"
"You're amazing, Pippa!"

Every year for her birthday, Pippa wanted more than just a party. She wanted a "Hooray for Pippa" parade. Pippa loved attention. It was like being in a spotlight.

Normally, after her birthday parade, Pippa went home and filled her belly with all the pupsicles and pupcakes her doggie heart desired.

On her fifth birthday, however, Pippa's human parents walked into the room with a gigantic, perfectly wrapped package.

"Pippa, we have a surprise for you."

Pippa bounded around, imagining a new crown for next year's birthday parade, a new tutu for her dance recital, or a sequined collar. But as Pippa tore into the gigantic, perfectly wrapped package, she realized there was one very small, very plain package inside.

"Pippa, this present will change everything for you." Sadly, Pippa eyed a small, yellow T-shirt with the words **BIG SISTER** on it.

For the next few months, as Pippa's mom's tummy grew bigger, Pippa's time in the spotlight grew smaller.

"When is the baby coming?" people asked, barely noticing Pippa in a new tiara. They also asked Pippa's mom other questions, like "Are you having a boy or a girl?"—all while Pippa twirled in her tutu to get them to pay attention to her. If they talked to Pippa at all, it was only about the new baby.

As the baby's arrival drew near, Pippa's share of the spotlight shrank even more.

"Quiet, Pippa, Mom needs to rest now."
"Stop, Pippa, you're twirling too close."
"Don't, Pippa, those are for the baby."

As the spotlight got smaller and smaller, Pippa's anger got bigger and bigger.

There's one more important thing to know about Pippa. Like some very special dogs named Owen and Lucy, Pippa had a job. She worked at a yellow house where children came when they felt sad and afraid and angry—and lots of other feelings too.
So Pippa understood feelings.

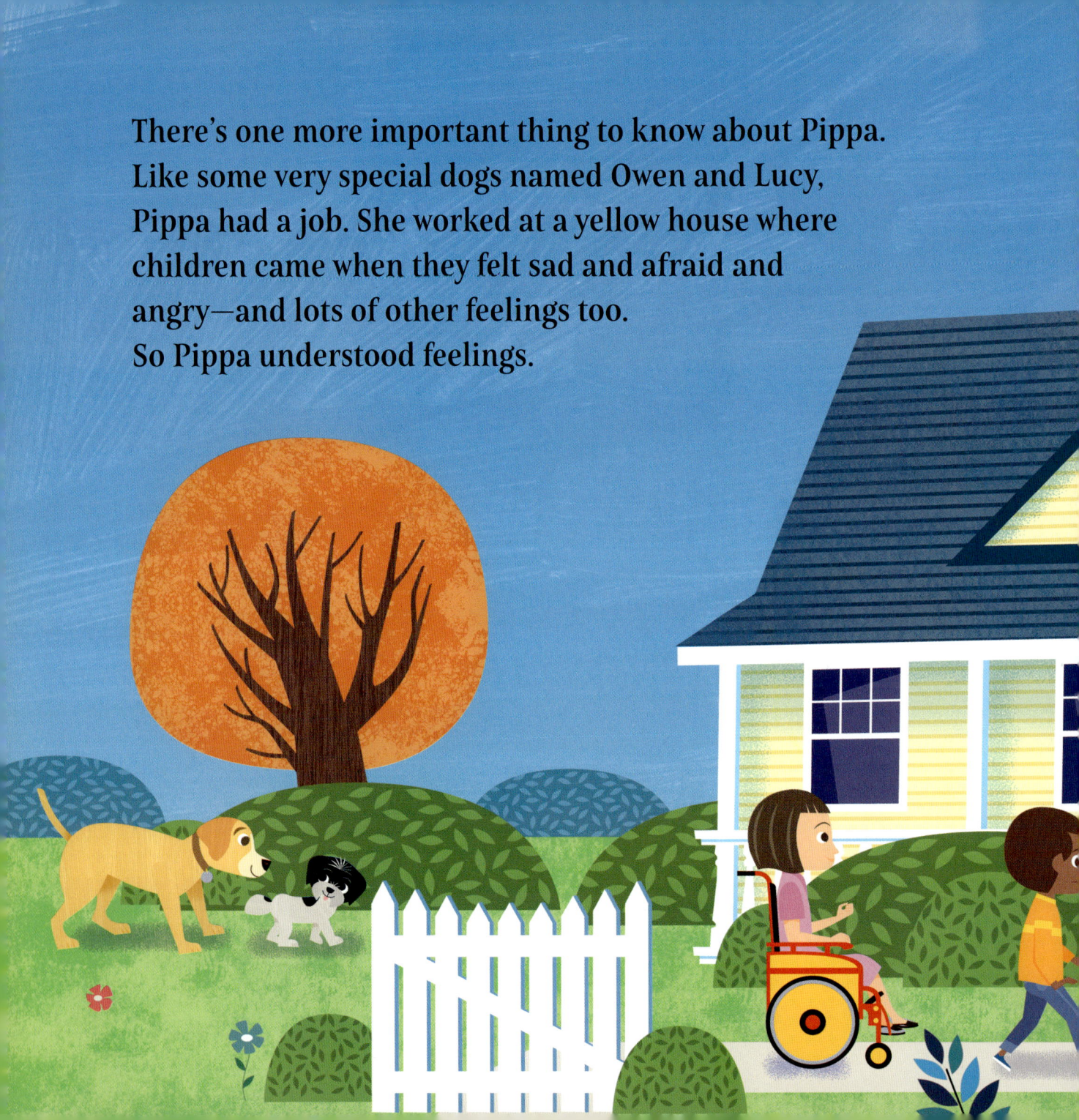

In the yellow house, they sometimes describe feelings using colors.

There are primary colors, like red, blue, and yellow. And those colors can mix together to form new colors, like red and yellow make orange. Or blue and red make purple.

Have you ever thought of your feelings as colors?
What color would you use for happy?
For sad? What about for angry?

Pippa's color for jealousy was a deep, brownish red because it was a mixture of two other feelings: the bright red of anger darkened by the green of fear. Feelings do that, just like colors. Sometimes they are by themselves and sometimes they blend with others.

Pippa was angry because people only talked about the baby who was coming soon. And she was afraid that her parents might love the baby more than her. So Pippa felt jealous sometimes.

On other days, though, Pippa felt happy and yellow. On one yellow day, Pippa felt like the queen of the household while her parents were away for a few days. Mimi and Pops were taking care of her, and they let her have parades EVERY day. Not just on her birthday.

But a turn of the doorknob changed everything.

The baby had arrived! She was cute, but when she cried, Pippa growled. "No, Pippa. Go lie down," her dad said.

Whenever the baby cried, Pippa tried to keep the brownish red away. But she still felt afraid. And angry. A jealous growl still escaped every so often.

But Pippa's parents were proving they had enough love in their hearts for both Pippa and her sister.

And Pippa was learning about the love in her own heart.

One day, something extraordinary happened. Pippa was wearing last year's birthday crown and dreaming about the next one. The baby was crying again, and Pippa's mom was doing everything she could to stop the crying.

Pippa began twirling, and the baby began laughing. The more Pippa twirled, the more the baby laughed.

"Pippa!" said her mom. "I couldn't get the baby to stop crying, but you did."

A few nights later—the night before Pippa's sixth birthday—the baby was crying again. Pippa peeked into her crib to see what was going on. When she put her head close to the baby, the baby fell right to sleep.

Just then, Pippa's parents walked into the room. "Pippa, you really are the big sister your little sister needs. Thank you for taking such good care of her."

The next morning when Pippa woke up, she had an idea.
Maybe her sister would want to join her in the birthday parade!

Pippa had learned that love is bigger than fear. And anger. And jealousy. The love she felt for her family—including her little sister—not only was stronger, but also made her feel better.

Pippa loved being a big sister. She had so much to share with the baby—crowns, tutus, parades, and even the spotlight.

# Helpful Conversation Starters

Tell me about a time when you felt celebrated.

Can you remember a time when the spotlight shifted to someone else? How did you feel?

What color would you give sadness? Anger? Worry? Happiness?

Who is one person you would like to share the spotlight with? How could you do that?

# To Parents and Caregivers—

Teaching kids to name their emotions is the best way to help them develop emotional intelligence.

With young kids, we start with the basics, using simple language and emotions like mad, sad, and happy. We then move toward an idea called *emotional granularity*, which involves more specificity. Think of it like a crayon box. Starter boxes have only a few colors and big, easy-to-grip crayons. Next is the two-row box, and kids learn there is more than one type of blue. Then comes the box with four rows and a built-in sharpener, and kids see there are actually multiple shades of every color. Emotions are the same way. This progression allows kids to start recognizing emotions like disappointment, jealousy, and worry.

The feelings wheel shown here can help teach emotional granularity.* It starts with basic emotions and radiates out to other emotions we want kids to learn. There are more detailed versions of feelings wheels, but for now, when you notice a strong emotion in your child, gently guide him or her to name a more specific aspect of that emotion.

Practice this the same way you practice bike riding and swimming with them. These aren't skills they develop overnight. Learning these skills can be more difficult for some kids and less so for others. And to maintain these skills, they have to practice them over and over. Remember that practice makes progress.

\* Adapted from "The Feeling Wheel" developed in 1982 by Gloria Willcox.